MYTHICAL CREATURES

A TALE AND SONGS OF TERRA INCOGNITA

KEVIN J. ANDERSON

WFP
WORDFIRE PRESS

Mythical Creatures: A Tale and Songs of Terra Incognita

Cover design by Miblart; Cover artwork image by Lee Gibbons

Kevin J. Anderson, Art Director

Published by
WordFire Press, LLC
PO Box 1840
Monument CO 80132
Kevin J. Anderson & Rebecca Moesta, Publishers

WordFire Press Editions 2025
Ebook edition ISBN 978-1-68057-792-1
Dust-Jacket Hardcover Edition ISBN 978-1-68057-794-5
Trad Paperback Edition ISBN 978-1-68057-793-8

Printed in the USA
Join our WordFire Press Readers Group for
sneak previews, updates, new projects, and giveaways.
Sign up at wordfirepress.com

CONTENTS

UNCHARTED SHORES LYRICS

WORDS AND MUSIC

Terra incognita. The unknown and uncharted lands beyond the edge of the map.

As a wide-eyed kid, I was always fascinated by the exploration of the world—the Age of Discovery, and old maps where wistful geographers would draw imaginative continents. They'd add dire warnings of "Here Be Monsters."

In college, when studying the history of the Middle Ages, I was enthralled by the legend of Prester John and his Christian kingdom beyond the horizon, a large undiscovered land of the faithful. In variations of the story, Prester John possessed the Holy Grail or the Fountain of Youth.

After the Moorish invasion of Iberian Peninsula from Africa in the early Middle Ages, Christian kingdoms fought against the Islamic armies for centuries, trying to drive them out of Europe. A persistent legend arose that if only the Christian kingdoms could find the land of Prester John, surely that great and powerful king would become an ally, send his Christian armies, and drive the Moors out of Europe.

This myth was, in part, the impetus for the Age of Discovery in the 15th and 16th Centuries, when Prince Henry the Navigator and others launched sailing ships with intrepid captains—Ferdinand Magellan, Vasco Nuñez de Balboa, Christopher Columbus, Batholomeu Dias, Vasco da Gama. Yes, those expeditions were to search for wealth and trade routes, but they were also looking for the kingdom of Prester John.

What a great starting point for a fantasy epic!

That idea seized me and wouldn't let go. After studying the complex history of the Crusades and the Age of Discovery, and reading many variations of the Prester John myth—even *Baudolino*, Umberto Eco's literary historical novel about Prester John, I realized that no real history could tell the tale I had in my head. I wanted more freedom.

The story would be vast, magical, and meaningful, and I needed to write it my way.

I loved stories of sea monsters, the kraken, the leviathan, merfolk, sea witches, and giant serpents. I also loved the swashbuckling adventures of Sinbad the sailor and countless other nautical legends. I could use elements from all of them and weave together a real epic. This story was going to be so good!

Next, I had to immerse myself in research about sailing ships, seafaring lore, and nautical knowledge. I visited the historic tall ships in San Diego Harbor. On a trip to Australia, I sailed around Sidney Harbor, I toured the fabled Shipwreck Coast near Melbourne, and spent a day in the amazing

Nautical Museum in Perth. On a Mediterranean cruise, Rebecca and I went to many sites from the Crusades as well as some of the great harbors of the Middle Ages.

Terra Incognita kept getting bigger and bigger. My trilogy would be a sprawling story like "Game of Thrones," with my own lands, cultures, and magic systems. I developed the history, geography, cultures, and religions. I wanted to tell a grand story of two continents and two religions at war, inspired by the Prester John myth.

But what if the clashing lands and religions—the equivalent of Christian Europe and Muslim Arabia—*both* had the same myth? A glorious land beyond the horizon, ruled by a powerful demigod like Prester John. If only they could find him, surely he would fight on *their* side.

And so, in Terra Incognita, each continent dispatches their sailing ships in search of the land of Terravitae, ruled by the powerful Ondun. Both lands have brave sea captains willing to face storms and sea monsters to find the promised land.

As a theme, I wanted to focus on religious hatred and intolerance. I have been appalled throughout history at the bloodshed and blindness caused by religious fanatics willing to commit countless atrocities in their belief that God was on their side and no one else's. From the song "Spiral" on the album *Terra Incognita: A Line in the Sand*: "You killed our fathers, so we kill your sons. How can you say you're the innocent ones?" It was a tit-for-tat-for-tit-for-tat, an endless spiral of revenge.

In writing Terra Incognita, I was adamant that each side believed that they were the heroes, that their actions were justified, while they remained blind to any compassion or justification on the other side. The story is heartbreaking and tragic, but also extremely powerful.

In all, I spent more than fifteen years researching, developing, world-building, and plotting this trilogy. Rereading all three of the books in preparation for this new edition, I was reminded of how much I had invested in this world. I don't know that I could ever do something so massive again. It is truly the grandest fantasy epic I have ever written.

AND NOW, THE SOUNDTRACK...

Rock music has always been a huge influence and inspiration on my writing. I can't play an instrument or sing, but I can *listen*. And the music and lyrics can spark many stories in my head. Over the course of my career I have written prominent projects with Neil Peart, legendary drummer and lyricist from Rush, but also other stories, books, and comics with Grammy Award-winning singer Janis Ian, Dan Reed (Dan Reed Network), and the bands Coheed and Cambria and Dream Theater.

One of my smartest high-school decisions was to join the Columbia Record Club. I lived in a small town in Wisconsin—far too small to have a record store—and I was at the mercy of American Top 40 radio from Chicago's WLS. But I wanted the kind of music that really spoke to me.

The Columbia Record Club sent solicitation packets through the mail, and I would always thumb through them. If you signed up for the club, you could choose twelve albums for a dollar. They sent sheets of little stamps, each showing an album cover, and you tore off and stuck the albums you wanted.

As a nerdy high school kid with thick glasses, hand-me-down clothes, and a bad haircut, I didn't have much interest (or luck) in finding girlfriends, so all those songs about lost love and bad breakups weren't very relevant. I had, however, read *The Lord of the Rings, Dune,* and lots of comic books, so I was delighted to discover offerings by the Alan Parsons Project, *I, Robot* and *Pyramid*, Styx's *The Grand Illusion*, Rush with *2112* and *A Farewell to Kings*, and Kansas with *Leftover-ture* and *Point of Know Return*.

Those albums filled my head with incredible songs about alien starships and dystopian futures, robot revolutions, voyages to black holes, and UFO encounters with ship captains on the open seas.

I'll never forget how inspired I was by the magnificent cover art for Kansas's *Point of Know Return*—an old sailing ship about to plunge off the waterfall at the edge of the world, and the back of the album depicts glorious sea serpents. I wanted to tell the story of that!

Later, as I became successful with my writing career, I was always on a parallel track with rock music, and I made no secret that those groups were the source of many a story or novel. My first novel, *Resurrection, Inc.*, was closely inspired by the Rush album *Grace Under Pressure*, and every song became a scene or a chapter. When *Resurrection, Inc.* was published by Signet Books in 1988, I acknowledged the three members of Rush and blindly mailed signed copies off to Mercury Records.

About a year later, I received a letter in response from Neil Peart, Rush's legendary drummer and lyricist. That sparked a friendship and creative collaboration that lasted more than three decades. For our first project together, Neil and I wrote the dark-fantasy story "Drumbeats" together based on his bicycle explorations across Africa, which was published in a paperback anthology.

But I always felt there was something more we could do to connect rock music and fiction. When I wrote my SF novel *Hopscotch* in 2001, Rush heavily influenced the storyline. While I was developing the book, I tried to encourage Neil to write lyrics that would cross over in the other direction, influenced by *Hopscotch*, but our timing wasn't quite in sync. (I wrote novels much faster than Rush produced albums.) And then tragic events in Neil's life made us shelve the entire idea.

Later, Neil really enjoyed my multi-volume space opera The Saga of Seven Suns, and he worked in multiple Seven Suns references into the lyrics for their *Snakes and Arrows* album.

It wasn't until 2010, though, that we finally succeeded in a novel and album collaboration. Neil had started developing the lyrics and story of the Rush concept album *Clockwork Angels*, which was to be the band's last studio album. Neil picked my brain about the steampunk genre, in which I had written several novels, and as the album progressed, he asked me to write the novel version of the album.

To me, this project felt like the pinnacle of my career! At last, the marriage of a rock album and a novel, produced simultaneously and influenced by each other during the creation. I was thrilled to the core about the project. I've written in many huge best-selling universes, such as Star Wars, Dune, X-Files, Star Trek, Batman, and Superman, but this felt like the biggest thing ever.

I took the proposal to my agent, who offered it to my major publishers. At the time, I had over 20 million books in print in 32 languages, with more than 50 national or international bestsellers. For their own part, Rush was a massively successful band with more platinum records than any other group in music history. They were preparing to go on an international tour for the *Clockwork Angels* album, one of the biggest acts on the touring circuit with sold-out shows in huge arenas. And they intended to sell the *Clockwork Angels* novel at the merch stands alongside the t-shirts and program books.

This project was a match made in heaven. It was a no-brainer.

To my chagrin, all of my major publishers—with whom I had published numerous bestsellers—offered only lukewarm responses, at best. "How do you write a novel based on a rock album?" And, "Do Rush fans even read?" They just didn't get the concept!

Hold that thought for later.

So, Neil and I published *Clockwork Angels* with his Canadian publisher ECW Press, who *did* "get it." They published a gorgeous edition of *Clockwork Angels,* which hit the *New York Times* Bestseller list its first week out, received rave reviews, and won several awards. Neil and I followed up with a companion/sequel, *Clockwork Lives,* and then plotted a final grand summation of everything we wanted to do,

Clockwork Destiny, which I had to write by myself after Neil's death in 2020.

Meanwhile, for years, I had been developing and working on my epic fantasy trilogy Terra Incognita, and I never gave up on the idea of doing a rock album in conjunction with one of my novels.

Over the years, I had built up friends and connections in the music industry, one of whom was Shawn Gordon, owner of ProgRock Records. I'll let him describe how we met:

"It was long long ago, in the before time, when MySpace ruled the land. I was a huge KJA fan and a huge Dune fan. I found Kevin's MySpace page, looking for information on when the next Dune novel was coming out. Then I noticed that Kevin had very similar musical tastes, and since I owned a record label that had many artists in that genre, I took the chance to message Kevin and offer some CDs as a 'thank you' for all the hours of enjoyment his books had brought. Kevin responded and accepted the offer, and so the CDs were shipped.

"A couple of weeks later, Kevin messaged back that he hadn't had much hope for the CDs, but they turned into some of his favorite material ... and would I be interested in talking on the phone about an idea he had?"

So, I pitched him my idea of an album connected to a new novel, and he was interested. When I told him how Terra Incognita had initially been inspired by the cover of the Kansas album *Point of Know Return*, he knew just what I was talking about. We threw out pie-in-the-sky ideas about how a concept album could feature songs about some of the characters and storylines—the perfect soundtrack.

At one of my Dune book signings in San Diego, a guy came up to the table with a bag of Dune books to be signed; he wore a t-shirt with a Dream Theater logo. Spotting it, I said, "Hey, I recognize that symbol!" It was Shawn Gordon, whom I had never met in person. After the signing, we adjourned to a local craft brewery and spent hours talking more in depth about a Terra Incognita crossover album.

From that point, it was inevitable.

He and I discussed the performers I really liked, the characters and storylines I wanted to highlight in an album. I blocked out the songs and the progression of the tracks.

I wanted the sea captain, Criston Vora, one of the main characters of the trilogy; his wife, Adrea, who is kidnapped in a coastal raid and taken back as a house slave of the rival Soldan; Captain Andon Shay, an old, hard-bitten sea captain who sets off on a doomed voyage; and the Soldan himself, Omra.

I drafted the lyrics for the songs, figured out a general idea of how I wanted each track to sound, and my wife, Rebecca Moesta—who has a much better poetic and lyrical sense than I do—cleaned them up into beautiful songs. Meanwhile, Shawn hired master keyboardist Erik Norlander, whose work I already loved, to write the music and record the tracks. His wife, Lana Lane, is a superb female vocalist, and I knew she would be perfect as the voice of Adrea.

James Labrie, the lead singer from Dream Theater, was the voice of Soldan Omra; John Payne from the supergroup Asia was the salty old sea captain Andon Shay; and Michael Sadler from SAGA was the main lead, Criston Vora. I knew

Michael's voice from SAGA's fast, upbeat tunes, but he absolutely blew me away with his the yearning, heartbreaking vocals on Terra Incognita. (To this day, I can't listen to "Letters in a Bottle" off the first album without getting a tear in my eye.)

Shawn also found other great performers, including David Ragsdale, the violinist from Kansas; Gary Wehrkamp from Shadow Gallery on electric guitars; Chris Brown from Ghost Circus on electric and acoustic guitars. We also had Mike Alvarez on cello, Kurt Barabas on bass, Chris Quirarte on drums, Martin Orford on flute, and of course Erik Norlander on keyboards.

Erik wrote about the project, "I really enjoyed working with the whole team and especially Kevin and Rebecca. I have been a lifelong Dune fan, so Kevin's deep connection to that rich universe gave us some instant creative common ground. All of the instrumentalists were stars: Gary, Kurt, David and both Chrises. For the vocalists, I already of course had a lot of experience working with Lana Lane and with John Payne, so that part was easy. But James LaBrie and Michael Sadler were two vocalists that I never thought I would find myself writing for, and this really pushed my compositional style in a very welcome way. Both of these gentleman took the project extremely seriously and gave it their full professional commitment. I think the results speak for themselves."

Lana Lane recently recalled working on the project, "This was a great experience working with so many talented and positive artists. I've worked on several ensemble cast albums in the past, and I always have some trepidation about how my voice is going to be mixed or set in an arrangement. I never had any of these concerns with this project. It was super high quality right from the beginning."

Though the overall project was going to be called Terra Incognita, we needed a name for our *band*. While we writing some of the songs, Rebecca and I happened to be on a vacation down to Roswell, New Mexico. I emailed Erik Norlander from our hotel room, brainstorming band names. Lana Lane also has a song about Roswell on one of her albums, and we thought, since there were six of us involved at the time, why not call the group "Roswell Six"? That one stuck.

The first album, *Beyond the Horizon*, came out from Prog-Rock Records as a companion to the first Terra Incognita novel, *The Edge of the World*.

When I began writing the second big novel in the trilogy, *The Map of All Things*, I got right to work on the next album. Due to other commitments, Erik and Lana weren't available to work on it, and Shawn turned to prolific songwriter Henning Pauly. I knew his work on Chain and Frameshift.

While *Beyond the Horizon* has a solid classic prog-rock feel to it, like Kansas and Emerson, Lake, and Palmer, the second album has more of a modern Dream Theater vibe. Henning says, "This album was extremely challenging, but I am very proud of the end result and how the music underlines the story!"

My friend Janice Ian, Grammy award-winning singer of the classic "At Seventeen" (which epitomized the lives of nerds and outcasts, teenagers like me) even assisted us with lyrics on two of the songs. Michael Sadler came back on the second album with equally beautiful vocals for a more tragic version of Criston Vora. Award-winning Canadian vocalist Sass Jordan is the new character of Queen Angine. Nick Storr from the Third Ending sings Angine's friend and love, Mateo.

As a real coup, Shawn secured Steve Walsh, the lead singer from Kansas, to voice an older Soldan Omra. This was a triumph and epiphany for me to have the man who sang "Carry On, Wayward Son" and "Dust in the Wind" provide vocals for my songs. Steve Walsh and Kansas, with *Point of Know Return*, were foundational influences in the entire trilogy.

Terra Incognita was the biggest fantasy epic I had ever written. These amazing albums with legendary performers made the trilogy unique in the field, unlike any other book series ever published.

The trilogy had a major publisher, and I had numeous bestsellers and awards under my belt. In my career I had a proven connection to rock music, given my obvious work with Neil Peart from Rush. I had two concept rock albums tied directly to the novels. This project was a match made in heaven. It was a no-brainer.

Recall what I said above about how old-guard publishers didn't really know how to think outside the box.

The Terra Incognita publisher and marketing team just didn't see any advantage to the crossover with the albums. We received coverage in the music press and even a feature in *Prog Rock Magazine*, but the book publisher did not participate in any cross-promotion with the music industry. To my knowledge, they never even mentioned the existence of the albums in their press releases.

The publisher felt I was better known for science fiction than fantasy, so *The Edge of the World, The Map of All Things,* and *The Key to Creation* were published only in paperback. Especially in those days in the publishing world, if a book wasn't released in hardcover, it got very little review attention in the trade magazines.

Terra Incognita was meant to be my magnum opus, which I'd worked on for fifteen years, but although the books were extremely well received by my reader base, they certainly didn't break any sales records.

I moved on to other ambitious projects, such as more Dune novels with Brian Herbert, a sequel trilogy to my Saga of Seven Suns, my Dan Shamble, Zombie P.I. series, and two more Clockwork novels with Neil Peart.

The Terra Incognita books became harder and harder to find,to the point where I had to scrounge used bookstores just to get extra copies for myself. Prog Rock Records went out of business, and while the songs were still available on some streaming services, it was nearly impossible to find the physical albums.

Fast forward ten years.

Although I still write new books for major traditional publishers, I've also become quite successful as a mid-sized publisher myself, mainly concentrating on reissuing nice editions of my own titles and continuing my favorite series.

My beloved Terra Incognita was out of print and even the audiobooks weren't available, so I had my agent initiate the process of getting the rights back. (Don't hold your breath.) Two more years passed with no response.

In the meantime, I got to know Bob Madsen from The Highlander Company Records, whose group The Grafenberg Disciples produced an amazing and touching tribute song, "No Words," after Neil Peart's passing. (Look it up on YouTube. I promise it's worth your time.) Bob was a big fan of Terra Incognita.

He took a motorcycle trip from California to visit me in Colorado Springs. During a hike together in the wondrous Garden of the Gods park, Bob asked me why I had never done the third and final Terra Incognita album. He hinted that he might be interested in helping make it happen.

As you might guess, the original project—while creatively amazing—had been something of a disappointment to me, considering the huge amount of effort and expense we had put into it. My ambitious novels weren't available anywhere, but I still didn't have the rights back (just the sound of crickets from the publisher). ProgRock Records was no more, and the first two CDs were very difficult to find. I didn't see much point in doing a third album, which would be an orphan upon release.

But then a miracle happened. Unexpectedly, I received a letter from the original publisher formally reverting all rights to Terra Incognita, including the audiobook rights. Now I could finally do this huge epic in the way I had always envisioned.

It was game on!

I contacted Bob Madsen and asked if he was still interested in working with me on the third CD. He was. (I'll let

Bob go into much greater detail from his point of view in his essay which follows.)

Back when *The Key to Creation* was originally published, having hope and faith that we would do the third album, Rebecca and I had drafted a set of lyrics, but they'd been shelved for a dozen years. Now I dusted them off and approached them with a fresh eye, while Bob worked on the music in his studio with his songwriting team Billy Connolly and Jerry Merrill.

Next, I set the wheels in motion to buy back the first two albums so I could remaster and reissue those CDs as part of the beautiful new Terra Incognita set. Shawn Gordon was glad to help see that the albums get back out to listeners.

We contacted the great Michael Sadler to reprise his role as Captain Criston Vora, ready to take one last voyage of redemption—and he delivered another stunning performance. Michael wrote, "....When I was first invited to be a guest vocalist on Terra Incognita: Beyond the Horizon (2009), the initial installment of Kevin J. Anderson's trilogy with Roswell Six (produced by Erik Norlander), I was unfamiliar with Kevin's work—let alone that he was a prolific, award-winning author—or what a privilege that invitation would become. I was thrilled to return for Terra Incognita: A Line in the Sand (2010) (produced by Henning Pauly), diving deeper into this musical saga. Finally, I had the honor of contributing to the third album, Terra Incognita: Uncharted Shores (2025) (produced by Bob Madsen), rounding out an incredible voyage. It's been my absolute pleasure to be part of this epic fantasy trilogy, and I'd like to extend my heartfelt thanks to Kevin and

Rebecca Moesta, the talented producers—Erik, Henning, and Bob—and the many gifted musicians who came together to make Terra Incognita the true masterpiece it is! Sail On!"

Then Bob and I worked with our mutual friend Dan Reed from the Dan Reed Network and convinced him to sing Prester Hannes, the evil fanatic (although in person, he is one of the sweetest, calmest people we know). Many listeners know Dan's voice from his funk rock in the 1990s, but here he was absolutely perfect with his dark and shaded performance.

For the female role of Ystya, an innocent demigoddess who doesn't know her powers, I suggested Dutch vocalist Anneke van Giersbergen, best known for her work with The Gathering, but I fell in love with her voice in her partnership on the song "Somewhere" with Sharon Den Adel from Within Temptation (in my opinion, the best duet of all time). To sing the part of the young sea captain Saan, Criston Vora's son, Bob enlisted Ted Leonard from Spock's Beard and Pattern-Seeking Animals.

The final song, "Not in My Name," was Bob's addition— when the rival ships finally reach the uncharted continent and meet Ondun (the Prester John figure), things don't turn out as expected. This powerful song is delivered by Hans Eberbach from Grafenberg Disciples—the very man who sang the Neil Peart tribute "No Words," which is how I got connected with Bob in the first place.

For amazing violins throughout the album, Jonathan Dinklage gave a virtuoso performance; I know Jonathan well from from Rush's *Clockwork Angels* tour and the "Bubba

Bash" Neil Peart tribute concerts; he also tours with Lady Gaga and Barbra Streisand.

On drums, we have Greg Bissonnette from the David Lee Roth Band and the Ringo Starr Experience, as well as Ed Toth from the Doobie Brothers and Vertical Horizon, and Jeff Tuttle from the California-based Rush tribute band Rash. Electric guitars are by Billy Connally, with additional guitar work from Jay Tausig and Jeffrey Wynn Price. Keyboards are by Jerry Merrill, background vocals by Emily Lynn from the world-renowned Australian Pink Floyd Experience, and Bob Madsen himself plays bass.

As one last Easter egg, my dear friend Doane Perry from Jethro Tull gives an impressive soliloquy on the final track as the voice of God himself. Doane is well-known as the drummer for Jethro Tull, but he has a rich, resonant voice, perfect for the part—and when I asked him to be the voice of God, how could he refuse?

We gave him the words to record, and this was the absolute last piece we needed before the final mixing of the album. Doane prepared to record in his home studio—just as the LA wildfires hit. His house was within a hundred feet of the evacuation zone, and his electricity and internet kept going in and out. I contacted him and told him not to worry about recording his piece, that we could do without it, that he should pay more attention to packing up and evacuating! But he insisted on doing it, saying that if the fires came and his studio burned to the ground, then this would be the last thing recorded there. He delivered in spades, and his voice sounds perfect in the song. Fortunately, his house escaped the fires.

So that's the full background of the Terra Incognita project, words and music, an epic story that I think is as powerful and relevant now as ever. Many people poured their heart and soul into all aspects of this multimedia project.

I hope you enjoy the novels and relish the accompanying music as much as I do. Set sail and join me on a voyage to wondrous lands unknown.

—KJA
Monument, Colorado

What happens when a close-minded prester is confronted with a mythical creature that his faith will not let him believe in?

MYTHICAL CREATURES

The prow of the *Compass* cut the rough gray waters like a knife carving a Landing Day roast. Prester Ormun closed his eyes and drove away all his pleasant memories of the traditional holiday ... or any other family memories, for that matter. Those were behind him now; only bleak settlements on the scattered Soeland Islands lay ahead. The prester had a difficult path to follow, even if he did not understand God's reasoning behind it.

The ship's damp sails creaked and sighed, and he felt the cold spray on his face, blown by the coming storm. Dobri, the bright-eyed cabin boy, came up beside him, leaning over the bow to peer down into the choppy waves. "Are you looking for *sylkas*, Prester? They say sometimes you can see them in the whitecaps just before a squall."

"I do not believe in *sylkas*. And neither should you." Prester Ormun knew that for a young man like this, the world was filled with mysteries and wonders, but also ignorance. It was his appointed task to enlighten the people of the islands.

The cabin boy squinted at the sea, which looked leaden under the thick sky. "They're real, Prester—beautiful women with golden hair or seaweed all over their bodies. Other sailors have seen them."

"I don't care what other sailors say. *Sylkas* do not exist. It is written in the Book of Aiden that God created the peoples of the land, but only fish, seals, whales, and sea serpents inhabit the sea—no intelligent creatures. I can show you the Scriptures, if you like." Since Ormun knew the cabin boy couldn't read, the proof would be lost on him.

Dobri was both disappointed and skeptical to hear the prester's pronouncement. He had grown up in a small fishing village, and this was his first voyage away from home; he wanted to believe all the wondrous, imaginative stories, whether or not they were true. Now the boy gazed ahead, intent on spotting one of the imaginary *sylkas* so he could point out the creature to Ormun.

With a pang, the prester realized that his own son Aleo would have been about Dobri's age now....

A large wave gushed over the *Compass*'s bow, and the cabin boy scuttled away, but the prester did not try to avoid the splash; instead, he let it wash away his past again. His family was gone, and nothing remained for him in the city of Calay. That was why he'd been sent across the rough waters to the bleak Soeland Islands. A new chance ... a last chance.

The church's prester-marshall had sent Ormun to preach among the roughshod and hardy islanders; he would bring them the Book of Aiden to comfort the people in their storms and cold northerly winds. Ormun accepted his first mission with neither enthusiasm nor complaint. He was humble enough not to expect redemption, but he did hope to achieve something positive with whatever remained of his life. That he was all he asked God for....

Back in Calay, before he became a prester, Ormun was a shoemaker with a wife and two children, a home, friends—a lifetime ago, or a year ago, depending on whether he measured time by a calendar or the gulf in his heart.

The gray plague had swept through the Craftsmen's District, as it did every few years. Shops closed their doors and latched the window shutters. But Ormun had his family to feed: his son, his daughter, and his wife, a dark-haired, tan-skinned beauty named Risula. And so, he kept working, while others hid.

He never knew which customer exposed him to the plague. Ormun lay shivering in bed for days while his family tended him: Aleo, only twelve years old, acting as the man of the house, Risula giving him salty broth to drink; even little Essa brought him flowers that she'd picked outside.

Ormun gained strength day by day, then suffered a relapse, falling back into a deep fever, sleeping like the dead, drenched in cold sweat. His last murky memory was of Risula shushing their daughter and leading her away, telling her to let her father sleep. And then his wife had started coughing....

When his fever broke, Ormun emerged from his coma, very weak, and he could barely open his crusted eyes. His throat was parched, and he called out for water, but heard nothing. The house seemed quiet, much too quiet. After he gained enough strength to crawl out of bed, he found his family huddled together, dead, victims of the fever that he had somehow survived.

Ormun had walked away from his home, wandering the streets in a daze, until he finally came upon the kirk. He stumbled inside, and the local prester cared for him, read to him from the Book of Aiden. It was then Ormun decided what his mission in life must be. The gray plague had left him with an empty heart, no laughter, and no love. He clutched onto his service to the church like an anchor of hope, read the Book several times through, and debated with great fervor. When the kindly local prester could no longer answer his questions, he sent the gaunt and intense Ormun to the main kirk in Calay, where he met with the prester-marshall himself.

Cast adrift in life, Ormun begged the church leader for a new course to set. The prester-marshall did not try to explain God's personal message for Ormun, didn't pretend to reveal the purpose behind all the pain he had suffered. "I know a place where you can be of service. The Soelanders need you, and I think you belong there." He anointed Ormun a prester and presented him with the Book and the fishhook pendant that was a symbol of their faith.

No one called Soeland a pleasant place to live, but that mattered not a whit to Ormun. He took his Book and his letters of passage, and begged a bunk on the *Compass*, which was ready to sail back for the islands....

Now the sea grew rough, and waves rocked the vessel. Captain Endre Stillen came to join the prester, looking troubled. He was a red-bearded man with a muscular chest and potbelly as hard as a wine cask. "Your cabin would be more comfortable, Prester. No sense staying out here in the storm —the weather is going to get worse."

"Discomfort doesn't bother me, Captain," Ormun said.

Stillen shot an uncertain glance to the anxious cabin boy who hovered nearby. "Dobri says that you don't believe in the mysteries of the sea." He raised his bushy eyebrows.

"I do not."

"The ocean is vast and uncharted, and we've all seen things we can't explain. I'm as inclined to believe in *sylkas* as in anything else. If nothing else, it gives me hope to know that those dark waters might contain benevolent creatures, should anything happen to my ship."

"I don't need mythical creatures to give me hope, Captain. The Book of Aiden says that *sylkas* don't exist, so therefore they don't exist. It doesn't matter what tales you've heard or what you think you've seen."

The conversation reminded Ormun of a recent outspoken stargazer who had adapted a seaman's spyglass so he could stare at the stars and planets in the night sky. The astronomer convinced himself that he saw tiny satellites circling one of the planets—an impossible idea. To prove his assertion, the stargazer had asked the prester-marshall to observe for himself; but the church leader refused to raise the spyglass to his eye. "The Book of Aiden tells us that God made the world as the center of all things, so therefore other satellites *cannot* circle one of the tiny planets in the sky. I have no need to look, when I already know." He handed the telescope back to the baffled astronomer. Ormun thought it was an amazingly profound demonstration of the prester-marshall's unshakable faith. He only hoped he could be as worthy someday.

Seeing that the prester's mind was set, Captain Stillen chose not to pursue the argument. "Those legends are a vital part of Soelander life and folklore, Prester. You'll be in for some lively discussions when you get to the fishing towns, that's for certain."

"I'm not afraid of debate."

The captain ordered the sails trimmed against the squall. As the winds picked up, waves hammered the side of the ship. Most of the crew hurried belowdecks before the rain started to sheet down.

Dobri yelped, pointing off to starboard. "I saw one! Look, Prester—it's a *sylka*!"

Ormun froze, wanting not to look, *almost* strong enough to refuse, but he couldn't help himself. He turned to where the boy pointed—and that was his weakness, his failure.

While he looked in the other direction, a rogue wave swamped the bow and gushed over the rails with enough force to knock him overboard. He reached out, grabbed for anything, and his fingers caught the slick wood, but couldn't get hold. Then the rush of curling foam bore him overboard into the wide gulf of the sea.

Prester Ormun sucked in a breath to shout for help, but he swallowed a mouthful of salt water instead. Flailing, sinking, he coughed and retched as the wave crest bore him upward, then plunged him under again. He clawed at the water with his hands, seeing grayish light above. His face burst from the waves again, and he drew in a deep breath.

He rose and sank, completely lost, adrift. His heavy woolen shift pulled him down.

In the pouring rain he spotted Dobri and Captain Stillen struggling to their feet on the deck. He caught a glimpse of the cabin boy, his mouth open in dismay as he saw the prester in the water. Dobri waved and shouted.

Ormun raised his hands to signal, but the seas were too rough. Currents whisked him farther from the ship. The *Compass* could never send out a boat to rescue him.

He tried to stay afloat, but his arms and legs felt leaden. His shoes—good leather boots that he had made in his own cobbler shop long ago in that other life—filled with water. He was going to drown out here.

Oddly, he didn't view the thought with any particular terror, but he did feel a heavy confusion. God's course for him had been so clear—to spread the word out in the Soeland Islands. What was the purpose of saving Ormun from the gray plague only to let him be swept away by a capricious wave, drowning before he even had a chance to preach to his new charges?

He went under again, struggled to the surface, caught another breath. Letting go, he let himself be flung about by the waves. Barely able to think, he experienced a paradoxical sense of calm and peace.

Then clammy hands grasped him from below. A firm grip took his woolen shift, cradled his head, buoyed him up to where he could breathe. But Ormun didn't want to breathe. He struggled and fought against the strange figure below, but he was too weak.

In the end, he simply surrendered to the water and the

mythical savior that his imagination had created in his last moments of life. Prester Ormun sank into the darkness, trying to remember a prayer.

WHEN PRESTER ORMUN AWOKE, he smelled fish in the dank and cold air around him. Dried saltwater plastered his hair to his head, and he had to pry open his crusted eyes. Before his vision adjusted, he rolled over onto his knees and retched, puking up foul-tasting saltwater.

He saw that he was in an empty cave at the waterline, which looked out upon the open sea. Outside, the waves sounded like drumbeats against the algae-encrusted rocks that he could see beyond the cave opening. With a start, the prester realized he was naked, his woolen shift spread on a rock nearby. The cloth was stiff and salt-encrusted, but reasonably dry. He shivered and pulled his clothes back on, hiding his nakedness.

He noticed four gutted fish on a flat rock next to him, along with a pile of oysters and clams, all of which had been pried open, ready for him to eat. Weak and starving, Ormun devoured the food without thinking, without tasting, and he felt reborn, as when he'd emerged from his fever after the gray plague. Now, however, questions clamored in his mind, and he looked around, trying to understand what had happened to him.

A figure swam in the sea outside the cave. It seemed human at first—until the creature hauled itself onto the rocks and climbed dripping into the cave. Covered with luxurious locks of golden fur, it was obviously female, with rounded breasts covered by matted weeds. The face was narrow and ethereal, with large brown eyes—soulful eyes, like those of a sea lion. She smelled of salt from the sea. Her lips curved in what was an unmistakable smile as she saw him awake and looking at her.

Ormun squeezed his eyes shut and felt for his fishhook pendant in a protective instinct, but the religious symbol was gone. Perhaps it had washed away when he'd been swept overboard, or perhaps this *thing*—this *sylka?*—had stolen it, fearing the sign of Aiden.

Ormun opened his eyes again, but the creature was still there; he had expected her to vanish like a mirage-shadow. She came forward to squat near him, briny water trickling from her fur, and he struggled away. The *sylka* picked up the empty oyster and clam shells and cast them out of the cave, then she turned back to scrutinize him, like a raven fascinated by a shiny object ... or a predator deciding how best to devour its prey. A thrumming sound echoed from her throat, a call that was at once mysterious, mournful, and hypnotic.

When the creature edged closer, Prester Ormun backed away until his shoulders struck the cave wall. "You're not real!"

The *sylka* trilled at him. Her eyes showed a yearning to communicate. She repeated the sound and chirruped with a higher note at the end, like a question.

"You're not real." Though he could see the *sylka*'s form as if she had been sketched from the logbook of a delusional sea captain, could smell her musky iodine odor, and hear the sound she made, Ormun clung to what the Book of Aiden taught: That God had blessed *mankind* with intelligence, giving only His *chosen children* the minds to understand and worship Him. All other creatures of the land and sea were lowly animals. In another verse, the Book specifically denounced mermaids and *sylkas* as distractions for a devout man, superstitions unworthy of a true follower of God.

But now Ormun found himself faced with the contradiction. The Book of Aiden stated plainly that this *sylka* could not be here. Ormun had read those words of scripture with his own eyes ... yet those same eyes showed him this impossible creature. Right here.

Back in Calay, the prester-marshall had instructed him in the use of rational thought. If this *sylka* truly existed, then the statement in the Book was in error. A small error, perhaps—and how could anyone know all the mysteries and all the creatures in the vast sea?

Yet one error in one verse was as bad as a thousand errors, for either way it proved that the Book of Aiden was flawed.

And because it was the word of God, the Book of Aiden could *not* be flawed. Therefore, that one verse, and all verses, had to be correct. By definition.

Hence, the *sylka* could not exist, and she was not there. He stared hard at her, willing the illusion to go away.

The *sylka* hunkered down and continued to gaze at him with mournful eyes. She let out a series of complex musical trills, but Prester Ormun closed his eyes and covered his ears.

∽

THE *SYLKA* LEFT the cave several times throughout the day, diving into the sea and swimming away. She always returned with fresh fish, oysters, or abalones for him, all of which he ate suspiciously. Ormun used the empty abalone shells to capture dripping water that trickled from the moist rocks of the cave. It tasted gritty and dirty but soothed his parched throat.

Each time the mythical creature went away, Ormun tried to convince himself that she was only an illusion brought about by delirium, perhaps a relapse of the gray fever. Then the *sylka* returned, and they would stare at each other again....

He feared she might bring back others of her kind to show them the strange captive she had hauled from the stormy seas—but, again, the prester knew that couldn't happen, because *sylkas* did not exist. There were no others. Each time she came to him, she was alone ... and so was he.

When he felt strong enough, and desperate enough, Ormun made his plans and waited for the *sylka* to swim away again. The creature slipped out of the cave one afternoon, and Ormun decided it was time to escape—if he could. He ventured out of the opening and climbed up on the rocks, hoping to find some landmark that would tell him where he was.

If this was one of the Soeland Islands, Ormun could make his way inland, where he might find people—a fishing village, a shack, or a boat dock. But when he scrambled up the algae-covered boulders above the tide line, he saw that this island was merely a tiny patch of land, an elbow of reef that barely rose above the waterline—a few acres of forlorn boulders and tufts of misplaced grass. He could see the full swatch of land from end to end, side to side. The island was empty. He was alone.

Staring at the watery horizon with tears burning in his eyes, he discerned the gray hummocks of other islands in the distance, larger shores that might be inhabited ... but they were much too far away. He could never swim that far, and if he tried to escape, he was sure the *sylka* would come after him, grab his legs, and drag him beneath the water. He still didn't understand why she had saved him in the first place.

As he stood there in empty dismay, the *sylka* rose out of the surf and climbed onto dry land on the other side of the islet. Silhouetted in daylight, she looked like a seductress, her form voluptuous, the golden kelplike fur haloed by the sun. Ormun had looked at women once, had found Risula so lovely that she made him dizzy with desire ... but he had been a different man before the gray fever—someone without the same convictions, without the same priorities. He averted his eyes.

The *sylka* came toward him, clearly alarmed to see him out of the cave. On land, her movements were ungainly, like a seal's, although he had seen how sleek and lissome she was in the water. When the creature urged him back to the cave that was his prison, he recoiled at her touch, but could not resist. He saw no point to it; he had nowhere else to go.

Back in her lair, the *sylka* was intent on showing him something. She trilled, inducing him to come to a dank alcove in the rear of the small cave. Under a weed-covered overhang, she had piled rocks to create a protective barrier, a sort of nest. The *sylka* looked at him with great wonder in her eyes as she grasped the rocks with her webbed hands and lifted them away one by one.

Beneath the protective barrier rested a group of pulsating, grayish spheres, pearlescent objects, each one larger than a ripe melon. Ormun counted five of them grouped together with loving care, moist with a filmy membrane—a clutch of eggs! The creature's young. She was reproducing, about to unleash five more of her kind into the world!

Obviously the *sylka* wasn't entirely alone out there in the waters. Ormun imagined her out in the gray cold sea, at night, letting out her trilling song, calling a mate from across the waves. Did she lay her eggs here in the cave and wait for a male to spray his milt on the clutch like a frog? The very idea made him shudder with disgust.

The *sylka* inhaled and exhaled wet burbling breaths, and she crouched closer, cooing. The creature extended a pale finger and stroked the nearest egg. Her touch activated something within, a sparkle in the air accompanied by the smell of ozone, and Prester Ormun felt an overwhelming sense of importance and hope—a magical, unnatural connection.

On the egg's shifting metallic surface, he saw distorted images, like memories seen through the fever fog. The *sylka* touched a second egg, and a third, and more images formed on their reflective shells ... the prester's hopes and possibilities from the lost part of his life, things she could not possibly know about him.

Ormun saw the blurry, uncertain features of his son Aleo, laughing, full of tales of fish he had caught or beetles he had collected. The second eggshell displayed sweet, doe-eyed Essa, who loved to pick the flowers that grew in meadows just outside the city. And exotic, beautiful Risula.

But the last time Ormun had seen his family, they were dead, plague-ridden, their bodies huddled on the floor of their home, while he shivered in a coma on the narrow bed. Now, he gasped a quick, perfunctory prayer, but he continued to look. He knew he should turn away, even though those faces made his heart ache.

Sensing his reaction, the *sylka* trilled with happiness.

Then Ormun realized these visions were not just memories, for he saw Aleo as a young man, standing with a thin and pretty red-haired woman. They held each other, kissed —Aleo's wife-to-be? Ormun saw another maiden with fresh-picked flowers in her hair, unmistakably Essa, just at the edge of growing up. He saw Risula cradling another baby —her own, or a grandchild?

The eggs held possibilities, a wellspring of the future.

"No," Ormun whispered, drawing away. "No, this never happened! This can't be." He covered his eyes. The *sylka* was distraught, not understanding his reaction, but Ormun clung to strength within.

The images that pooled on the shells of her eggs did not represent the path that God had chosen for him. He had endured the pain. He had read the Book. He had fought for understanding and acceptance, like a pathfinder hacking through persistent underbrush, rather than taking a simple and easy trail that did not lead where he wanted to go. These elusive memories were not *his* memories, and that future did not belong to him.

"No," he said again.

With obvious disappointment, the *sylka* piled the rocks again over her eggs.

EVEN THOUGH THE prester understood his mission now, he feared he wouldn't have the necessary strength. As he shivered through the cold, damp night while wrestling with his thoughts, Ormun once again told himself that none of this was *real*. Maybe he had actually drowned when the wave swept him overboard, and this was his test before God let him enter Heaven. The only thing that had kept him alive after the plague, the purpose that allowed him to get through one day, then the next, was the anchor of his faith, his dogged belief in what the prester-marshall had taught him. If he abandoned that, then he would be abandoning everything he had left.

The eerie, tempting images he'd seen in the *sylka*'s eggs —his family, his happiness, a bright future—none of that was true. How he longed for what he saw in those illusions, wanted that reality more than anything else he could ever imagine. But that, in itself, was what warned him. *His* wishes did not matter: It was about what God wanted. Ormun had to be strong, and his only strength was his faith.

On the fourth morning after being washed overboard, Ormun watched the *sylka* return to the cave, climbing out of the water. As the creature sloshed toward him, she looked excited, gesturing with a webbed hand. When the prester didn't follow, she hurried back to the cave opening and stared out to sea, then trilled a sharper sound, more urgent than her soothing music. Ormun felt compelled to look out upon the sunwashed waters.

In the channel between the islands, close enough that he could see the sails and rigging, a two-masted vessel cruised in from the north. He even recognized the lines, the look of the hull, the cut of the sails. It was the *Compass*! Maybe Captain Stillen had come back to look for him, or maybe this was just the ship's regular return route through the archipelago.

Thrumming, the *sylka* looked at him with her limpid eyes. Ormun's heart lurched, and he knew the time had come. This was the crux, and he clung to the truth like a man grasping a lifeline. He had not dared to pray for a chance at redemption, to demonstrate his devotion and his acceptance—and now the sailing ship had returned! The *Compass* would rescue him.

He lurched to his feet, uttering a prayer of thanksgiving. The *sylka* gestured for him to hurry, and by her demeanor and bright expression he guessed that she intended to swim out to the *Compass*, draw the attention of the sailors, and get Captain Stillen to change course to the islet. This creature had already rescued him from drowning, and now she would save him from being marooned on the small island. She turned away, looking out to sea.

Ormun picked up one of the melon-sized reef rocks, held it in both hands, and brought it down with all of his strength on the back of the *sylka's* head. He bashed as hard as he could, and her skull was much softer than the rock.

The *sylka* collapsed, letting out a mournful hooting sound, and Ormun struck again.

He stood tall and dropped the rock on the floor of the cave. "You don't exist." If the captain, the cabin boy, and the rest of the crew saw her, they would not have the strength to cling to their faith. Ormun had no other choice but to save them from their own gullibility.

He went to the back alcove, pulled away the rocks piled over the clutch of eggs, and gazed down at the quicksilver pooling—the reflections that were mocking echoes of a past that was already gone and a future he would never have. Useless and dangerous, a mocking temptation. Prester Ormun was strong enough to avoid fantasies, no matter how attractive they might be. He knew his life's course.

Ormun picked up another rock and smashed the first *sylka* egg, obliterating the illusions of things that might have been. Then he destroyed the rest of the clutch, one by one, until he felt safe again.

When he was finished, he was surprised to discover that the *sylka*'s body still lay on the cave floor; the dripping slimy fragments of broken eggs remained strewn about their nest. Now that he had passed his test of faith, Ormun expected them to vanish instantly, but he didn't search for, or want, explanations. It was time for him to be rescued, to return to his role as a prester preaching the Book of Aiden. The Soelanders needed him.

Ormun carried one of the abalone shells as he scrambled out of the cave and onto the high point of the small islet. There, he jumped and waved, seesawing his hands in the air, trying to get the attention of the *Compass*. He caught the bright sunlight with the shiny interior of the shell, flashing a signal. He yelled until his throat was raw.

And finally—finally—he saw pennants raised on the mainmast, and the ship turned toward the rocky island. Someone had seen him.

When the *Compass* anchored at a safe distance from the islet, Prester Ormun watched the ship's boat lowered, saw men rowing toward him. Though he was not a good swimmer, he dove into the water and struck out to meet the boat partway. He recognized the boy Dobri at the front of the boat, and two sturdy Soeland sailors pulling at the oars. The prester flailed in the waves, swimming as far from the islet as he could.

He needed to be away from the persistent imaginary remnants of the *sylka* and her eggs. He didn't want any of these men from the *Compass* to see the evidence, otherwise they would be deceived by what they wanted to believe.

Gasping and exhausted, Ormun reached the boat, and his heart swelled with joy. Dobri leaned over to catch his hand. "Prester, we thought you were dead!"

"I thought I was, too," he said as they helped to haul him aboard. "But I survived, and now I know that God still has more work for me to do."

The cabin boy laughed, and the sailors rowed back toward the *Compass*. Ormun was too tired and shaken to tell his story, and he still had much to think about before he revealed anything.

When they tied up to the sailing ship, he climbed aboard to congratulations from Captain Stillen. "We couldn't believe it, Prester! No man ever survives out here. How did you make it to that small island? We were just continuing our passage among the islands, but Dobri spotted the flashing light."

"An abalone shell," the prester said.

The captain admired his cleverness, and Dobri added, "I was at the bow looking for *sylkas* when I saw it."

"*Sylkas* don't exist, boy," Prester Ormun said, more convinced now than he had ever been.

But while the crewmen took him to change into dry clothes, the prester watched Dobri hurry back to the bow with a spyglass in hand. Seeing the boy's eager willingness to believe, he felt only sadness and disappointment. He had to teach these people the truth, no matter how difficult it was.

Nevertheless, Dobri continued to scan the waves, always looking, always hopeful.

BEYOND THE
HORIZON LYRICS

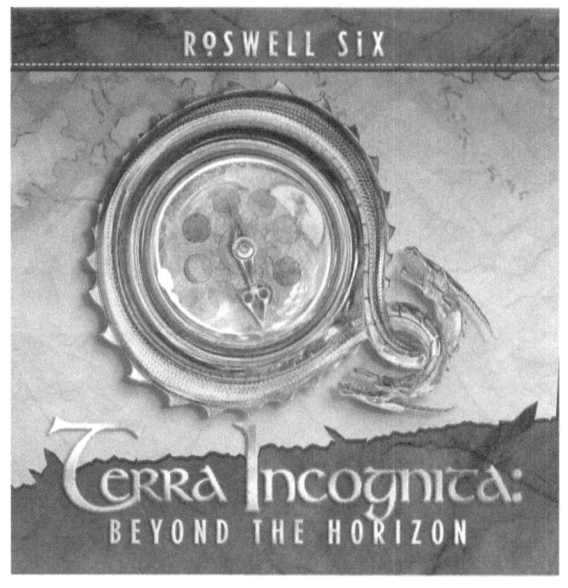

ISHALEM

Ishalem, Ishalem, Ishalem!

Omra
Ancient city of legends and hope
Ship upon a lost shore
Sacred faiths tied to one another
Strain against each other
Walls enclose and yet divide

(*Refrain*)
Sow the gold of glory
Feed the fires of faith
Claim the heart, the heart of truth
Reap the harvest of hate.

Ishalem, Ishalem, Ishalem!

Adrea
Streets are scoured clean by salty winds
Windows glitter like colored gems
Turrets sparkle with gold
Canals like silver ribbons
Lead us to the heart of all

(*Refrain*)
Sow the gold of glory
Feed the fires of faith
Claim the heart of truth
Reap the harvest of hate.

(*Bridge)*
Pilgrims journey to behold you,
Home of wisdom, pure and true,
Even eagles flying high
They can't see all your majesty.

Ishalem, Ishalem, Ishalem!

Criston
Towers rise beside the sea
Standing guard against our foes

Adrea
No merchant can buy you
No scholar can know you
No priest can bend your will

(*Refrain*)
Sow the gold of glory,
Feed the fires of faith,
Claim the heart of truth,
Reap the harvest of hate.

Sow the gold of glory,
Feed the fires of faith,
Claim the heart of truth,
Reap the harvest of hate.

Captain Shay
A careless spark and ready blame
Consume the ancient walls in flame.

Omra
And so the war begins. . . .

CALL OF THE SEA

(Criston)
What's out there to explore?
I really need to know.
I dream of golden shores
That's why I long to go.
And all ... I'll miss ... is you.
While every day it calls to me,
The Song of the Sea.

(Adrea)
Oceans are wide
Wide as my heart
Hearts hold dreams
Now follow yours
While we're apart

I'll dream of you
Let the waves of your dreams
carry you away,
then back home to me.

(Criston)
I yearn to see it all
Each wonder to behold
I must obey the call,
That echoes in my soul.
And all ... I'll miss ... is you.
And every day it calls to me,
The Song of the Sea.

(Adrea)
Oceans are wide
Wide as my heart.
Hearts hold dreams.
Now follow yours.
While we're apart
I'll dream of you.
Our dreams will keep you close to me
As you sail on the sea.

(Captain Shay)
All that you long for is out there—
Treasure, adventure, and fame.
Lorelei maidens with gold hair
Are already calling your name.

So drink in a breath of the fine salty breeze,
The scent of a rainbow, and ambergris
Come see the wonders with your very own eye --
When you reach the edge of the world, you can fly.

(Criston)
There's magic in each tide,
A spell upon the sea.
Beyond where charts can guide.
A new world waits for me
And all ... I'll miss ... is you.

(Adrea)
Oceans are wide
Wide as my heart
Hearts hold dreams
I'll dream of you....

The wind will blow your love to me
In the song of the sea.

Oceans are wide
Wide as my heart
Hearts hold dreams
I'll dream of you....

I AM THE POINT

(OMRA)

I am the point
I am the voice
I am the point...

I hear the crowds cheer.
I can taste their fear.
I see them look up to me.
The people believe in me.
I know what they want from me.

I—
I am the point—
The point of their lives
Their lives of desperation.

I am the point.

I hear your advice,
But I roll the dice.
I feel all your wants and needs.
I've seen what resentment breeds.
I know what you want from me.

I—
I am the point—
The point of your view
Your view of the world.

(Bridge)
I am the point—
The point of no return.

Am I wrong, am I right
To take up the fight?
I let no one choose for me.
I'm seizing my Destiny.
I know what I have to be.

I—
I am the point—
The point of the sword.
The sword that rules the world.

I—
I am your lord.
I am your voice.
I am the One.
I am the point!

LETTERS IN A BOTTLE

(CRISTON)

On paper, my words
My thoughts, my love.
I write for your eyes alone
The ink is smeared with a tear, my love.
My heart is lost without you.

Sealed in a bottle
Trusted to the sea
Borne on the waves that surround me.
May the currents and the tides
Be merciful guides
And bring this letter to you.

As winds on these dark seas take me far
I make a wish upon a star

And hope and I pray
These words will find their way
And you'll read this letter from me.

Sealed in a bottle
Trusted to the sea
Borne on the waves that surround me.
May the currents and the tides
Be merciful guides
And bring this letter to you.

With a strand of your golden hair
My love, may it find you there
This page is filled with yearning.
And all of my heart longs for you...

Bridge
Though I sail beyond the horizon
Though I hear the songs of tempting sirens
Only one voice calls my heart
Your love will bring me home

This paper holds a kiss, my love.
My fondest dreams, my bliss.
And all of my hopes and love, my love
In a letter I send to you.

HALFWAY

(ADREA)

I wake up each day
as I did before.
I do the same things
And I do them some more.
Seems like no one noticed
the change in my life.
It's the same
but different.
It's so different

My clothes are the same
I haven't changed my hair.
I go to work
and I try to care.
Why does no one notice
the change in my life?

It's the same
but different.

My mind is only halfway here,
My heart is always halfway there,
Because my other half is otherwhere.
He's otherwhere....

Bridge
Every hope that I had
sailed with him that day,
And 'til he's back at my side
I've tucked my dreams away.

It's so different.

I walk the same streets
and I greet my friends.
But my loneliness
never seems to end.
How could no one notice
this change in my life?
It's the same
but different.

My mind is only halfway here.
My heart is always halfway there,
Because my other half is otherwhere.
He's otherwhere....

It's so different.
It's so different.
It's so different.

Anchored

(OMRA)

My faith is an anchor:
It holds me and steadies me,
Keeps me secure.
I believe, I believe.

In what God has shown
In what prophets have known
In words carved in stone
I believe, I believe.

No current too strong
Can pull me along
Or weaken my song.
I believe, I believe.

Like light in a mirror
It couldn't be clearer
The truth draws me nearer.
I believe, I believe.

But those who refuse,
To honor our views,
What more can they lose,
If they don't believe?
Won't believe?

Their faith is an anchor
That drags them down
Until they drown
in the Truth.

I have been blessed
Above all the rest
I have a new quest.
I believe, I believe!
I believe, I believe!

My faith is an anchor
It holds me and steadies me,
Keeps me secure.
I believe, I believe.

HERE BE MONSTERS

(Captain Shay)
Here be monsters
   Dangerous reefs
Krakens prowl
   The darkest deeps
This is where
   Leviathan sleeps.

Ancient legends
   Recognize
Ship and treasure
   Fool and wise.
These are all
   Leviathan's prize

(Criston)
Don't know what's below
Don't know what's ahead
Don't know what's out there
But we sail to the edge—
    The edge of the world!

(Adrea)
Steer the right course
Let the compass guide
You'll find your way home in the end.

(Captain Shay)
Ships gleam gold
    As daylight breaks
Gallant captains
    Know the stakes
Ready when
    Leviathan wakes

Bold explorers
    Fearless roam
Sailing on a
    Path of foam
into old
    Leviathan's home

(Criston)
Don't know what's below
Don't know what's ahead
Don't know what's out there
But we sail to the edge—
    The edge of the world!

(Adrea)
Steer the right course
Let the compass guide
You'll find your way home in the end.

(Captain Shay)
Unknown seas
    Empty maps
Stirring serpents
    Thunder claps
Beware of
    Leviathan's traps

Thick clouds rise
    As black as hate
Warning of a
    Stormy fate
If we pass
    Leviathan's gate

(Criston)
Don't know what's below
Don't know what's ahead
Don't know what's out there
But we sail to the edge—
 The edge of the world!

(Adrea)
Steer the right course
Let the compass guide
When you reach the edge of the world,
 You can fly...

THE SINKING OF THE LUMINARA

INSTRUMENTAL

THE WINDS OF WAR

(ADREA)

It was a day like any other
Morning with blue skies
And then the storm came
And then the world changed.
How can you stop a flame
Blown by the winds of war?

Why did they come here?
What did we do?
Why do they hate us?
What can we do?
Torn by the winds of war.

It was a day like any other
The battle once far away
We see now first-hand
And like a firebrand

It consumes our land
Fanned by the winds of war.

Why did they come here?
What did we do?
Why do they hate us?
What can we do?
Torn by the winds of war.

With fire and fury,
With malice and hate,
They burn and they pillage,
They murder and rape.

Flashing their swords,
They carve out our fate.
We are the spoils of war.

It was a day like any other
Sunset with red skies.
The)storm has awoken
Our spirits are broken.
What more can be spoken
Above the winds of war?

Why did they come here?
What did we do?
Why do they hate us?
What can we do?

It was a day like any other...
And the end of our world.

We are the spoils of war.

SWEPT AWAY

(*Adrea*)
Swept away.
I couldn't stay.
It all happened so quickly.
Cruel hate,
Cruel fate
That took me from our world.

Well I don't know where you are,
But my heart is never far
Away from you.

(*Criston*)
Tempest force
Blown off course
It all happened so quickly.

Ruined now
I don't know how
You'll ever wait for me.

Though I don't know where you are,
Still my thoughts are never far
Away from you.

We're apart,
But in my heart,
I'm simply swept away.

(*Both*)
I'll dream of you,
I'll dream of you,
Long for you,
Long for you,
But time goes by so slowly
End of rope
At the end of my rope,
Dare I hope
Dare I hope
That love will find a way?

Now I don't know where you are.
But my hopes
            and dreams
            and love
            are never far

Now I don't know where you are
Away from you.

How can I bear another day
Away from you?
Away from you?

BEYOND THE HORIZON
(CRISTON)

Can't fill this hollow
With a swallow
    of wine.
No more bleakness.
It's a weakness
    to pine.

I need to find my destiny,
I'm searching for my destiny,
Beyond the horizon.
Beyond the horizon.

Light the darkness
Banish the starkness
    of grief.

Rescue ragged hope
from a jagged
      dark reef.

I'll sail to a new destiny
I know I have a destiny
Beyond the horizon.
Beyond the horizon.

She might be waiting there
Oh, will I find her there
beyond the horizon?
Beyond the horizon.

Quench the sorrow
My tomorrow
      is here.
Raise my eyes and
My horizon
      is near.

I'll sail to a new destiny,
Embrace my brand new destiny,
Beyond the horizon.
Beyond the horizon.

It's just waiting there
And I want to find it there
Beyond the horizon.
Beyond the horizon.
Beyond...

MERCIFUL TIDES

(ADREA)

On paper, your words, your thoughts, your love.
I read with a pleading heart.
The ink is smeared with a tear, my love,
For my life was lost without you.

Sealed in a bottle, a gift from the sea
Borne on the waves from you to me.
Ah, the currents and tides
were merciful guides,
To bring your letter to me.

As winds on dark seas took you far,
I made a wish upon a star,
And hoped and prayed
that you'd find a way,
To show you remember me.

Sealed in a bottle, a gift from the sea
Borne on the waves from you to me.
Ah, the currents and tides
were merciful guides,
To bring your letter to me.

Though I may have been taken far
To strange lands under distant stars,
I read your note with yearning.
And all my heart longs for you.

Though I'm lost beyond the horizon,
Like I'm stranded on a desert island,
Let my warm voice call your heart.
Let my love bring you to me.

Your warm embrace I miss, my love,
But this paper holds your kiss.
I feel all our hopes and love, my love.
In the letter you sent to me.

THE EDGE OF THE WORLD

INSTRUMENTAL

CREDITS

Lyrics by Kevin J. Anderson and Rebecca Moesta
Music by Erik Norlander

Vocals: James LaBrie, Michael Sadler, Lana Lane, John Payne.
Keyboards: Erik Norlander
Bass: Kurt Barabas
Drums: Chris Quirarte
Electric guitars: Gary Wehrkamp
Acoustic and additional electric guitars: Chris Brown
Violin: David Ragsdale
Cello: Mike Alvarez
Flute: Martin Orford

Originally produced by ProgRock Records, Shawn Gordon Executive Producer

A Line in the Sand Lyrics

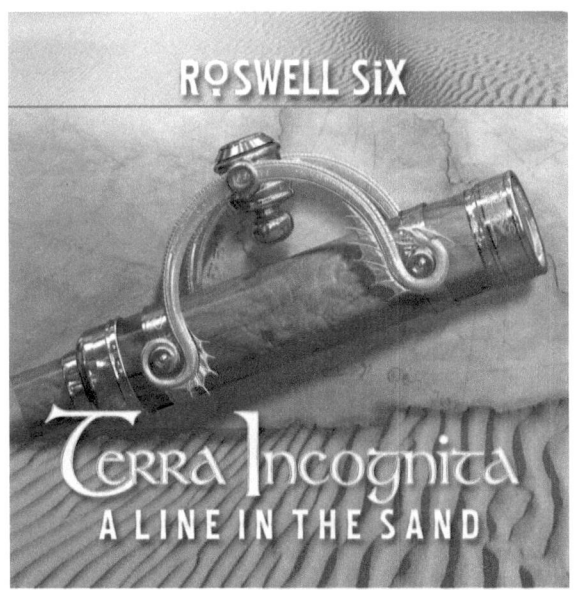

BARRICADE

(SOLDAN-SHAH OMRA)

A line in the sand,
A wall to the sky...
Barricade!

We don't need your kind with us,
So just stay on your side.
Every time you get too close,
Our principles collide.

We don't need you to agree,
Our faith is true and tried.
We will never think like you,
The gap is just too wide.

Chorus
Brick by brick
Stone by stone
We build the wall
To protect us all.
The faith that I had is long gone

Maybe you can't see the truth—
It makes no difference now.
We made a choice to still your voice,
Can live with it somehow.

We don't need a better view,
We've got the one we chose.
It may take ten thousand years,
to dam where the river flows.

Chorus
Brick by brick
Stone by stone
We build the wall
To protect us all.
The faith that I had is long gone
Long gone!

Bridge
One more brick, one more row.
We see less, the higher we go.
One more brick, one more row,
We don't need to look when we already know.

When we already know!

Don't try to reconcile with us—
Let's end this masquerade.
Can't hear you shout, when you're locked out
Behind this, behind this barricade.

Chorus
Brick by brick
Stone by stone.
We build the wall
To protect us all.
The faith that I had is long gone
Long gone!

Brick by brick
Stone by stone
We build the wall
To protect us all.
The faith that I had is long gone, gone, gone.
Long gone.

A line in the sand...

WHIRLWIND

(MATEO)

The storm has arrived.
The darkness is here.
Our dreams of tomorrow
Hold bloodshed and fear.
They won't disappear.
They won't disappear.

Chorus:
Somewhere in the whirlwind
We pray for the calm
We try to hang on
    We have faith,
    We seize hope,
    We hold love, we hold love, we hold...

Our nightmares are warning
Our hearts to be strong.
Survival's the only
True victory song—
So much could go wrong.
So much could go wrong. . . .

Chorus:
Somewhere in the whirlwind
We pray for the calm.
We try to hang on
    We have faith
    We seize hope,
    We hold love, we hold love, we hold...love.

Bridge:
The eye of the storm
Frames a moment of calm . . .
The world holds its breath for
The next sword to fall.

So startle the thunder
And shout down the storm.
Cling tight to each other
For life must go on.
    We wait for the dawn.
    We wait for the dawn.

Repeat Chorus:
Somewhere in the whirlwind
We pray for the calm
We try to hang on
    We have faith
    We seize hope,
    We hold love.

We pray for the calm
We try to hang on
    We have faith
    We seize hope,
    We hold love. We hold love, We hold love
    We hold love....

THE CROWN

(QUEEN ANGINE)

I was born in tradition
I know it is time.
I ask for no pity
The honor is mine

This is the place
I truly belong.
I carry the weight
My shoulders are strong.

Chorus
It raises me, it weighs on me
Liberates me, re-creates me.
It enthrones me, but it owns me
This crown I wear.

It will guide you, surely bind you

Terrify you, and inspire
It commands you, reprimands you
This crown I wear.

Verse
They say I'm too young
To wield so much power.
I wanted a life
Not this ivory tower.

My family, my kingdom
A part of my soul
The glory, the trappings
They all take their toll.

Chorus
It raises me, it weighs on me
Liberates me, re-creates me.
It enthrones me, but it owns me
This crown I wear.

It will guide you, surely bind you
Terrify you, and inspire
It commands you, reprimands you
This crown I wear.
This crown I wear.

Bridge
A circle of parts:
My hand and my heart
My land and my throne
My flesh and my bone
My mind and my soul
My self and my role
My light and my air
This crown I wear.

Verse
I accepted a kingdom,
  I surrendered my heart.
And I'm merely a woman.
  A true queen plays her part.
I could have been happy
  To love only one.
And now I must love them all,
  And that dream is gone.
  That dream is gone.

Chorus
It raises me, it weighs on me.
Liberates me, re-creates me.
It enthrones me, but it owns me.
This crown I wear.

It will guide you, surely bind you
Terrify you, and inspire.
It commands you, reprimands you.
This crown I wear.

It raises me, it weighs on me.
Liberates me, re-creates me.
It enthrones me, but it owns me.
This crown I wear.
This crown I wear.

LOYALTY

(MATEO)

I am used to victory,
And I don't say it pridefully
Nothing's worthy to me,
except what I offer.
Accept what I offer—
To you

Your people, they cheer and applaud.
Advisers will always agree.
But in your life
you don't need another fraud.
What you need is **honesty**
...a little honesty.

Chorus
A man should never surrender,
but I surrender to you.
I lay my tribute at your feet.
Just take what you need.

A man should never surrender,
but I surrender to you.
I give you my oath, my devotion, my creed—
My loyalty.

How could I offer you anything less
than everything you ask of me?
I will always be with you, always protect you.
And I'm proud to profess
My loyalty.

Chorus
A man should never surrender,
but I surrender to you.
I lay my tribute at your feet.
Just take what you need.

A man should never surrender,
but I surrender to you.
I give you my oath, my devotion, my creed—
My loyalty.

Bridge
What would I give, if you asked?
All my strength
All my dreams
All my days
And my years.
My blood
My heart, my life...
And my love.

Chorus
A man should never surrender,
but I surrender to you.
Lay my tribute at your feet
So take what you need.

A man should never surrender,
but I surrender to you.
I give you my oath, my devotion, my creed—
My loyalty.

My Father's Son

(SOLDAN-SHAH OMRA)

I will remember
I will be different
I won't make the same mistakes
I'll take a new path
Another direction
I won't, no I won't be my father's son
My father's son

My words
   Won't be so cruel
My rules
   Will make more sense
My life
   Will feel secure
My sons
   Will honor me
   Will honor me

Chorus
My father's son
That's what I am.
Or am I not?
Please tell me, god!

If that's what I am,
Will his mistakes
Be mine to make
If I'm indeed
My father's son?
My father's son!

Yes, I remembered
Yes, I am different
I don't make the same mistakes
I took a new path
Another direction
Trying not to be my father's son.

My words
   Are sometimes harsh
My rules
   Must be obeyed
My life
   Is just too full
My sons
   Are all renegades.
   Are renegades.

Chorus
My father's son
That's what I am.
Or am I not?
Please tell me, god!

If that's what I am,
Will his mistakes
Be mine to make
If I'm indeed
My father's son?
My father's son!

And so I remembered
I'm not so different
And I made my own mistakes
I forged a new path
Another direction
And I'll always be my father's son
...my father's son.

My words
My rules
My life
My sons

Could I be
My father's son?
That's what I am.

Or am I not?
Please tell me, god!

If that's what I am,
Will his mistakes
Be mine to make
If I'm indeed
My father's son?
My father's son!
My father's son!

WHEN GOD SMILED ON US

(MATEO)

Red was the flush of a young maiden's lips;
Now it's the color of blood.
White was a blanket of pure mountain snow;
Now it makes shrouds for our dead.

Bridge
A memory so faint
It gets harder and harder to find.
A memory that fades
Buried deep in my mind

Chorus
In happier days, we were at peace,
When God smiled on us,
Our hearts were content,
And our laughter flowed free,
When God smiled on us.

When God smiled on us.
When God smiled on us.

Churches once called down God's blessing on us;
Now, they cry out for revenge.
Trumpets blew fanfares proclaiming good news;
Now they call armies to war.

Bridge
A memory so faint
It gets harder and harder to find
A memory that fades
Buried deep in my mind

Chorus
In happier days, we were at peace,
When God smiled on us.
Our hearts were content, and our laughter flowed free,
When God smiled on us.
When God smiled on us.

Harmony
How much more will we bruise?
How much more can we lose?
How much more must we win,
Before God smiles on us again?

So...
How much more
   Faint
will we bruise?
   I can't
How much more
   Remember
can we lose?
   So
How much more
   deep
must we win,
   in my mind
Before God smiles on us again?
When God smiles on us again?

So, how can this be?
How can we get him to smile?
What must we do so that God smiles on us again?

A memory so faint
It gets harder and harder to find.
A memory that fades
Buried deep in my mind

In happier days, we were at peace,
When God smiled on us.
Our hearts were content,
And our laughter flowed free,
When God smiled on us.

And how much more must we win,
When God smiled on us.
Before God smiles on us again?
God smiled on us.

NEED

(QUEEN ANGINE)

In my heart, I stand alone
Even so, I always know
I can lean on you.
When I'm lying awake
With the whole world at stake
I still see you.

Chorus
Though it isn't all I want
And I know that it will haunt
me, I say,
I
I need
I need you
I need you to go.

I
I need
I need you
I need you to go.

You've seen me as I am
But I know you understand
I must play a part.
And you'd never betray
Any secrets that weigh
on my heart

Chorus
Though it isn't all I want
And I know that it will haunt
me, I say,

I
I need
I need you
I need you to go.

I
I need
I need you
I need you to go.

Bridge
How I want to let you in—
I can tell you see the signs.
There are words I cannot speak
So please read between the lines.
Between the lines...

We both know what we must do
This is what I need
what I need from you
to go on.
But my mind can't erase
Longing dreams of your face
while you're gone.

I
I need
I need you
I need you to go.

I
I need
I need you
I need you to go.

I
I need you
Need you to go.

I need
I need you

I need you....

SPIRAL

(SOLDAN-SHAH OMRA)

What do you achieve
With wounds that you leave?
You leave us to grieve.
We'll never forget what you've done to us.

The pain that you've caused
The lives that we've lost
The bloodshed you've cost
We'll never forget what you've done to us.

Chorus
You killed our fathers
So we kill your sons.
How can you claim
You're the innocent ones?

You killed our fathers
So we kill your sons.
How can you claim
You're the innocent ones?

Why should we feel shame
When you are to blame?
It's always the same,
In this unending game.

The hate in your soul
    The hate in your soul
Will burn and corrode.
    Will burn and corrode.
We take what we're owed.
    We take what we're owed.
We'll never forget what you've done to us.

Where does it begin
Original sin?
We can't let you win.
We'll never forgive what you've done.

Bridge
Action, reaction–
It's a spiral,
Spiraling out of control

Action, reaction—
It's a spiral,
Spiraling out of control

You killed our fathers
So we kill your sons.
How can you claim
You're the innocent ones?

You killed our fathers
So we kill your sons.
How can you claim
You're the innocent ones?

Why should we feel shame
When you are to blame?
It's always the same,
In this unending game.

Action, reaction—
It's a spiral,
Spiraling out of control

Action, reaction—
It's a spiral,
Spiraling out of control

BATTLEGROUND

INSTRUMENTAL

VICTORY

(MATEO)

Victory, victory, victory
Is ours
Victory!

Victory, victory, victory
Is ours
Victory!

Battle horns blow
and survivors are calling.
Mortal wounds flow—
how the mighty have fallen!
The land once was yours,
and now it is ours,
Paid for in blood
by the pawns of great powers.

Lived my whole life
based on honor and glory
But the battle today
was much more than a story.
We fought and we won,
and they lost and they died
Now the triumph at hand
shows that God's on our side!

Chorus
Victory, victory, victory
Is ours
Victory!

Victory, victory, victory
Is ours
Victory!

As they lie dying,
the weak and the brave
Corpses are mingled,
both soldier and slave.
But all blood is red,
and the dead ask me why—
In a war that won't end,
was it worth it to die?

Bridge
I choke as spilt blood drains my innocence dry.
Smoke, like their souls, rises faint to the sky.
Is this victory?

Chorus
Victory, victory, victory
Is ours
Victory!

Victory, victory, victory
Is ours
Victory!

[repeats]

Is this victory?

A line in the sand...

CREDITS

Words and Story by Kevin J. Anderson & Rebecca Moesta

Music by Henning Pauly

Steve Walsh—Vocals
Sass Jordan—Vocals
Michael Sadler—Vocals
Nick Storr, Vocals, Backing Vocals
Alex Froese, Vocals, Backing Vocals
Charlie Dominici, Vocals
Arjen Lucassen, Backing Vocals
Juan Roos, Backing Vocals
Henning Pauly—All Instruments, Backing Vocals

Originally produced by ProgRock Records, Shawn Gordon
Executive Producer

Uncharted Shores Lyrics

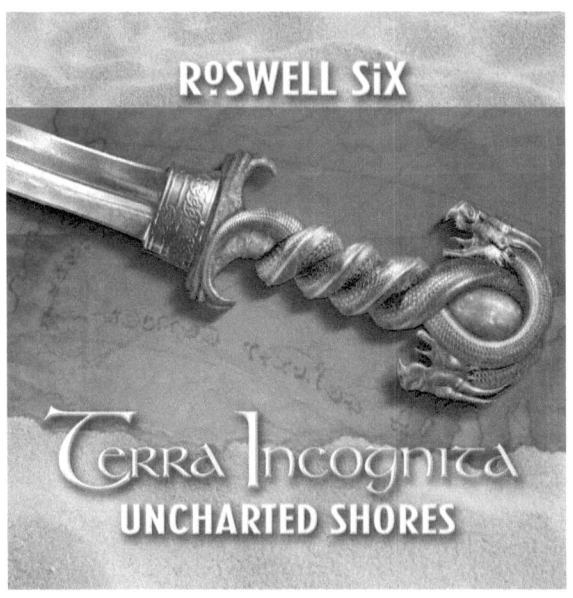

UNCHARTED SHORES

(CRISTON VORA)

I had a dream
Of life ever after
A wife, a home,
and children's laughter
I had a plan
I kept it all so simple
But I lost it all.

'Cause I was down on my knees
Losing hope by degrees.
Put my whole life behind me
Went where no one could find me

Where was the spark?
My heart wrung dry
It's so hard to start again

But there's still life left worth living
Yes there's still life worth living

Chorus
So I brave the waves
Ride the wind
I'm facing this world head on
And I'm ready for more!

There are wonderful magical worlds to explore
So show me more,
show me more,
show me more!
Farther beyond all I've known before.
So show me more,
show me more,
show me more!

And now I hold my head up high again
And I embrace the open sky again.
There are magical worlds to explore
And I know that there's got to be more

I brave the waves
Ride the wind
I'm facing this world head on
And I'm ready for more!
There are wonderful magical worlds to explore
So show me more,
Show me more,

Show me more!
Farther beyond all I've known before.
Show me more,
Show me more,
Show me more!

I'm headed on a fresh new course again
I'm open to a higher force again
I've been wasting the years
Giving in to my fears
When I could have discovered majestic frontiers

There are wonderful, magical worlds to explore
So show me more,
Show me more
Show me more.
Farther beyond all I've known before
So show me more,
Show me more
Show me more.

Sail on!
Yes, I will add to my story
Sail on!
For my land, my god, and for glory

And on uncharted shores
where no others have gone
We'll leave the first footprints
and greet the new dawn.

Sail on!

So show me more,
Show me more
Show me more.

So show me more,
Show me more

There are wonderful, magical worlds to explore
So show me more,
Show me more
Show me more.
Farther beyond all I've known before
Show me more!

THE PROMISED LAND

(SAAN)

We were promised a dream
of a far-off land
Where grass is always greener
The water always sweeter
The flowers bloom brighter
The whole wide world is wider
In the promised land

Chorus
I believe in dreams
I believe in promises
I believe in hope
I believe in love
The horizon holds

Promises dreamed
And promises made
Promises kept
And a promised land

Did we lose our motherland
For this tired old home?
Where skies are looking grayer
Our hearts give up on prayer
Our winter's getting bleaker
Our hearts are growing weaker
Is the promise lost?

I believe in dreams
I believe in promises
I believe in hope
I believe in love
The horizon holds
Promises dreamed
And promises made
Promises kept
And a promised land

We were promised a time
of legend and song
When smiles are glowing warm
When there's shelter from the storm
When our backs are never bowed
And our laughter rings out loud
In our promised land.

The horizon holds
Promises dreamed
And promises made
Promises kept
And a promised land

Bridge
I was sent to find that place
Long ago foretold
In maps of old
In sacred scrolls
A land full of wonder and grace

The land is what we make of it—
A paradise or a hell
Is the land we're leaving, someone else's
Promised land, as well?

The horizon holds
Promises dreamed
And promises made
Promises kept
And a promised land

The horizon holds
Promises dreamed
And promises made
Promises kept
And a promised land

The horizon holds
Promises dreamed
And promises made
Promises kept
And a promised land

SENSE OF WONDER

(YSTYA)

I used to look at the stars, cast my thoughts afar
And wonder ...
A sense of mystery filled our hearts—
Our night dreams,
and daydreams.

And the greatest wonder:
You showed me love
You gave me new life.
You made me imagine,
You gave me hope
You opened my eyes.

chorus
You've shown me countless wonders
Like grains of sand
Like stars in the sky

You pulled me out of my well,
You found my wings
And taught me to fly.
And then from out of nowhere ...
You gave me that sky!

I once was hidden away, isolated,
Could only wonder ...
I had questions, couldn't dream
Can't see rainbows through closed doors

And the greatest wonder:
You showed me love
You gave me new life.
You made me imagine,
You gave me hope
You opened my eyes.

chorus
You've shown me countless wonders
Like grains of sand
Like stars in the sky
You pulled me out of my well,
You found my wings
And taught me to fly.
And then from out of nowhere ...
You gave me that sky!

Just to be by your side
fires my heart and my mind
With wonder ...
With you I'll remain,
and live out the dreams
That we share. What's out there?

And the greatest wonder:
You showed me love
You gave me new life.
You made me imagine,
You gave me hope
You opened my eyes.

chorus
You've shown me countless wonders
Like grains of sand
Like stars in the sky
You pulled me out of my well,
You found my wings
And taught me to fly.
And then from out of nowhere ...
You gave me that sky!

You've shown me countless wonders
Like grains of sand
Like stars in the sky
You pulled me out of my well,
You found my wings
And taught me to fly.

And then from out of nowhere ...
You gave me that sky!

Smell the air
Hear the sea
We are free...
We are free...

Smell the air
Hear the sea
We are free...
We are free...

HAUNTED, HUNTED

(CRISTON VORA)

What if I could change the painting?
Add a detail, remove a shadow?
What if I said my goodbyes?
What if I confessed my love?

Wish I could make it different
Wish I could fix the errors
and stop the terrors
I wish that was my life.

Chorus
Haunted, hunted,
Oceans are vast,
Fleeing my past,
Running before the mast,
Haunted, hunted

Memories as deep as the sea
My past as dark as the waves
My course was lost in the storm.
Haunted, hunted.

Full circle, but could I escape?
Full circle, and could I survive,
Full circle, with sunrise ahead,
Let me sail round the world.

Chorus
Haunted, hunted,
Oceans are vast,
Fleeing my past,
Running before the mast,
Haunted, hunted

Bridge
Ponder the paths a man takes
What choices, what turns brought me here?
How can I pilot my life
My future, my heart, my love
Like debris on an uncharted sea,
Drifts together and drifts apart?
How can I pilot my life?

Chorus
Haunted, hunted,
Oceans are vast,
Fleeing my past,
Running before the mast,
Haunted, hunted

MORTAL ENEMIES

(PRESTER HANNES)

I am on a path, I know where I'm led
I am on a path, following the call
I am on a path, salvation lies ahead
I am on a path ... will I rise or fall?

Chorus
You push, I pull
You whisper, I shout
You deny, I affirm
I hold fast, you hold doubt.

But there's no doubt that my faith is strong—
And everything you know is ...
WRONG.
My faith is strong.

You are on a path that leads you astray
You are on a path, there is no reprieve
You are on a path, it won't help to pray
You are on a path. You have been deceived!

Chorus
You push, I pull
You whisper, I shout
You deny, I affirm
I hold fast, you hold doubt.

But there's no doubt that my faith is strong—
And everything you know is ...
WRONG.

We each took a path to the promised land
We each took a path trusting what we knew
We each took a path. Truth is close at hand
We each took a path—and I will stop you!

Chorus
You push, I pull
You whisper, I shout
You deny, I affirm
I hold fast, you hold doubt.

But there's no doubt that my faith is strong—
And everything you know is ...
WRONG.

Bridge
My faith is an anchor
A guiding star of hope.
Or is that light the fires of hell?
Either way, I'm going there!

It is my destiny
My prize
My reward
And my salvation
Is it my doom or my choice?
Either way it's all mine.

Chorus
You push, I pull
You whisper, I shout
You deny, I affirm
I hold fast, you hold doubt.

But there's no doubt that my faith is strong—
And everything you know is ...
WRONG.

But there's no doubt that my faith is strong—
And everything you know is ...
WRONG.

LIGHTHOUSE

(CRISTON VORA)

My lighthouse,
Showing me the way
And showing me home.

My lighthouse,
Showing me the power
And showing yourself.

My lighthouse,
Seeing what I need
And seeing who I was.

My lighthouse,
I see how to shine
And I see who you are.

High enough to see
Shining through rough seas
Far enough away
Perspectives that often change

For so long now I've looked up to you
Your soul doesn't waver,
You stand straight and true.
From close or afar, you've been my guiding star.
You are my lighthouse.

My lighthouse,
I see what I need
And I see who I was.

My lighthouse,
I see where I failed
And why I need you.

For so long now I've looked up to you
Your soul doesn't waver.
You stand straight and true.
From close or afar, you've been my guiding star.
You are my lighthouse.

For so long now I've looked up to you
Your soul doesn't waver.
You stand straight and true.
From close or afar, you've been my guiding star.
You are my lighthouse.

Bridge
A bright light calls to me
A silver siren song
Direction in the dark.
A spark in the storm

A view from on high
A sense of perspective
The compass of my heart,.
My life's direction.
My life's direction.

High enough to see
Shining through rough seas

For so long now I've looked up to you
Your soul doesn't waver.
You stand straight and true.
From close or afar, you've been my guiding star.
You are my lighthouse.

For so long now I've looked up to you
Your soul doesn't waver.
You stand straight and true.
From close or afar, you've been my guiding star.
You are my lighthouse.

THE BALLET OF THE STORM

INSTRUMENTAL

THE KEY TO CREATION

(YSTYA)

There's wonder in creation
You're searching for the key
In all of your exploration
What have you found
What have you found in me?

There's wonder in creation
You're searching for the key
In all of your exploration
What have you found
What have you found in me?

Do I make you afraid?
I'm still me in the end
If your fears are allayed
Will you make me
Will you make me your friend?

Do you love what you see?
Can you see who I am?
Do you want what you see?
Do you want who I am?

I'm the Key to All Creation

Dive deep beneath the surface
Look past the calm façade
You'll find we all have purpose,
And everyone
And everyone is flawed

A bud may hide a rose
A seed may hide a tree
An egg may hide a dove
What hides inside
What hides inside of me?

Do you love what you see?
Can you see who I am?
Do you want what you see?
Do you want who I am?

I'm the Key to All Creation

Bridge
Just close your eyes
Discard the lies
That dim the light
My heart shines bright

There's more to truth than vision.
Insight outshines precision.

Be my true confidant.
We could go hand in glove
'Cause I want what you want
Just to love and be loved

Do you love what you see? *(Still waters run deep)*
Do you see who I am? *(Still waters run deep)*
Do you want what you see? *(Still waters run deep)*
Do you want who I am? *(Still waters run deep)*

Do you love what you see? *(Still waters run deep)*
Can you see who I am? *(Still waters run deep)*
Do you want what you see? *(Still waters run deep)*
Do you want who I am? *(Still waters run deep)*

I'm the Key to All Creation

UNEXPECTED

(PRESTER HANNES)

I was taught,
I believed,
I had faith,
I didn't need
To question.

I knew the rules,
I obeyed.
Never swerved,
Never strayed
From my faith.
From my fear.

Am I the only one here?
Echo chamber loud and clear.

My heart is strong
What I know
Can't be wrong
How can I carry on
Having proved the truth right before my eyes?

This is so unexpected.

There are two
different views.
What I see
What is true.
For me I can't be wrong,
I am sure.

For so long
I've been pure.
I believed,
but I was blind.
Echoing loud and bold.
Dutifully do as I'm told.

My heart is strong
What I know
Can't be wrong
How can I carry on
Having proved the truth right before my eyes?

This is so unexpected.

My heart is strong
I have faith.
I belong.
How can I carry on?
How can I carry on?

No one expected me to do any good.
Did what I had to be
You would if you could.
Pouring fuel on the flame
Get on my knees and pray for rain.

No one expected me to do any good.
Did what I had to be
You would if you could.
Pour the fuel on the flame
Get on my knees and pray for rain.

NOT IN MY NAME

(ONDUN)

What part didn't you understand?
I said it with a clear voice.
The blood on your hands
Was not your only choice.
All the evil that you do
Was not part of my plan.

I say it again—
What part didn't you understand?

A simple story told by a simple man
It should have been so clear.
Paradise was always so near.

Not in my name!
Not in my name!
Not in my name!

I'm telling you
Not in my name!
Not in my name!
Not in my name!

You missed the moral of the story.
You missed the whole point.

Did I stutter?
Did I mumble?
Was something lost in translation?
The violence you do and the damage that you've caused.
Now you do unto others
Before they do unto you.

I say it again—
What part didn't you understand?

A simple story told by a simple man
It should have been so clear.
Paradise was always so near.

Not in my name!
Not in my name!
Not in my name!
I'm telling you
Not in my name!
Not in my name!
Not in my name!

You missed the moral of the story.
You missed the whole point.

Not in my name!
Not in my name!
Not in my name!
I'm telling you
Not in my name!
Not in my name!
Not in my name!

You missed the moral of the story.
You missed the whole point.

Spoken
It was a simple story
by a simple man
to love each other
and help if you can.
To learn and grow
And explore this land.
Where did it all go so wrong?

Children dying in the streets
Hatred on the face of all you meet.
Action, reaction—it is not a random interaction.
This was never the plan.

Not in my name!
Not in my name!

Not in my name!
I'm telling you
Not in my name!
Not in my name!
Not in my name!

You missed the moral of the story.
You missed the whole point.

(Lyrics by Bob Madsen)

CREDITS

Lyrics by Kevin J Anderson and Rebecca Moesta, with Bob Madsen
Track 10 lyrics by Bob Madsen.

Music by The Highlander Company Records "Wrecked Crew" of songwriters. (Bob Madsen, Billy Connally, and Jerry Merrill)

Michael Sadler—vocals
Ted Leonard—vocals
Anneke Van Giersbergen—vocals
Dan Reed—vocals and additional keys on tracks 5, and 9
Hans Eberbach—vocals
Doane Perry—spoken vocals
Emily Lynn—background vocals and arrangements
Jeff Tuttle—drums
Gregg Bissonette—drums

Ed Toth—drums

Bob Madsen—bass guitar

Billy Connally—electric guitar

Jerry Merrill—piano and keyboards

John Dinklage—violin/viola

Jay Tausig—nylon guitar

Jeffrey Wynn Prince—acoustic guitar

THANK YOU, MR. ANDERSON

BOB MADSEN

I n the 70's, for a scrawny, tow-headed, awkward kid with enough freckles to identify him as the loser in a Lilliputian paintball tournament, and someone who just couldn't seem to make friends, books were a godsend, a safe haven, and a wonderful way to while away the summer hours.

By the time I was twelve, I was a seasoned traveler. I had walked the snowy steppes of Cimmeria, dined under the trees in Rivendell, explored the dreaming Isle of Melniboné, wandered Barsoom and beyond. I had traveled to Gor (now, that author had issues!) and I'd sat at the Round Table in Avalon. If there was a passport for Sci Fi and Fantasy fiction, mine would have been overflowing with stamps from every-where and every epoch. I was also a well-versed comic book aficionado—X-Men being my favorite, of course—and I knew the origin story of just about every DC and Marvel comic character in circulation. Yep, I was a nerd.

I remember baby-blue curtains on a summer afternoon in the San Francisco East Bay with no air conditioner and me reclining on a Naugahyde couch. If you did it just right, you could build up a layer of sweat between you and the couch, which would stop you from ripping off your skin when you got up. From that couch I traveled the multiverse and the stars. It started with whatever books and comic books I could find from friends, then the dad of a friend down the street started letting me borrow from his collection. He was all kinds of cool. He had a membership to the Science Fiction Book Club—happy day!

All those stories in my head informed the man I am today. I became obsessed with storytelling, and because of that obsession I soon discovered Heavy Metal and Progressive Rock music. I loved bands like Rush, Yes, Genesis, UFO, Iron Maiden, and Black Sabbath, and then later, Planet P, SAGA, Marillion, and others. I loved listening to music that took you away to another place, told you a story, and made you think all the while.

I had started playing guitar at the ripe old age of seven, but it took until I was about fifteen to really find my instrument: "The Fisher Price Big Guitar for Stupid People," AKA the Bass. After that, there was no stopping me as I wrote song after song after song, emulating my heroes and trying to tell the stories that were bubbling up inside of me. I branched into Folk, Fusion, Funk, New Wave, and more. I simply couldn't get enough. Music and reading became two pillars of my life—pillars that, I'm happy to say, still stand at the corners of my existence to this day.

Anyway, enough of this trip down Memory Lane; on to the meat and potatoes. In 2011 I was finishing up the debut album for my band 41POINT9 (a Douglas Adams reference, for those in the know) and was casting about for a record label. Somehow, I was referred to ProgRock Records, and when I did my due diligence on the label, I saw three albums that convinced me that, hey, if they were good enough to have these guys on the label, they were good enough for me! Those three were Tony Carey (Planet P), Michael Sadler (SAGA), and this really cool rock opera by a supergroup named Roswell 6 that featured a slew of my Progressive Rock heroes. I eventually signed with ProgRock Records, but unfortunately the label folded shortly after the release of the second Roswell 6 album and my own debut of 41POINT9, *Still Looking for Answers.*

I had all three of the Terra Incognita books and got the two Roswell 6 albums and enjoyed them immensely. I went on to release an EP with Tony Carey under the name Operation Paperclip, and another—this time ill-fated—album with 41POINT9. But I always wondered why there wasn't a third album to complete the triumvirate of the Terra Incognita rock operas.

Fast forward about ten years, and I now had a new band, The Grafenberg Disciples, and Operation Paperclip had evolved to be a partnership with Dan Reed (Dan Reed Network). The Grafenberg Disciples had written and recorded a tribute to Neil Peart after his untimely passing, entitled "No Words."

Soon after the release of the video accompanying "No

Words," I got an email from someone thanking me for putting out the song and video, commenting that he felt he had been "punched in the gut and gotten a warm hug at the same time." I looked at the signature line and said, "Holy shit, that's Kevin J. Anderson!"

Needless to say, I wrote back thanking him for his comments. That email exchange was the start of a very nice friendship that has resulted in the two of us working on a feature-length sci-fi movie with Dan Reed (currently in production), a graphic novel in development, a music video for the most recent The Grafenberg Disciples record ... and lots of ribbing and laughter along the way.

In September 2023 I decided I needed a solo vacation, so I hopped on my BMW R1250 GSADV (Westside Beemer Boys Rule!) and headed east from Northern California with stops in Lake Tahoe, Las Vegas, Utah, and eventually made it as far as Colorado Springs, Colorado. There I met the Jedi Master himself, Kevin J. Anderson (cue the ominous orchestra music).

On a sunny fall morning Kevin decided to take me to the Garden of the Gods park just outside of the city. The Garden is something right out of an early Star Trek episode with red rock formations and paths and arches and columns—let's just say it's pretty trippy. It also happens to be at 6,400 feet (1,951 meters) of elevation! This Bay Area boy was gasping for air the whole time! I kept looking around for an oxygen mask to fall from overhead. Our conversation went something like ...gasp, pant, wheeze, "Yeah Kevin that sounds so cool!", gasp, gasp,wheeze, snort, cough, wheeze, "Then what did you do?" gasp, gasp (sound of a body crumpling to the ground) "No, don't wait up, I'll be right with you!" gasp, wheeze.... (Mind you, all this time Kevin is bouncing around from one rock to another like an overcaffeinated mountain goat, with nary a care in the world.)

Somewhere in the middle of all that starving for oxygen, I managed to ask him if he ever planned to finish that "Terra Incognita thingie." He rolled his eyes with a bit of an "Oy vey!" expression and replied that he had lost too much money and time on the project and that the previous publishers just didn't seem to get what was so cool about the album and novel combo. He had been trying unsuccessfully to get the rights back for quite a while.

I suggested that now might be the time to reintroduce the project, considering his increased exposure (Not that kind of exposure! Those records were sealed!) as a result of the Clockwork Angels trilogy with Neil Peart. He pooh-poohed my idea, and I gingerly left it alone, figuring it must be a sore spot for the guy. I said that if he ever changed his mind, I might be convinced to help, as I would really like to see the project finished.

We came out of the park and color slowly started returning to my extremities, eventually the blue tweety birds that had been circling my head faded from my eyes and we enjoyed a delicious lunch consisting of that favorite of stalwart mountain men ... Pizza.

The next night, after my lovely wife Daphne flew into Denver, Kevin and his wife joined us at a spiffy Brazilian restaurant (what Kevin calls "The Waterfall of Meat"). We all ate way too much and laughed way too much and basically had a good time.

A day or so later, after dropping Daph at the airport, I headed west just ahead of a major storm. I rode all the way at about a 45-degree angle to the road due to the wind, snow, and rain, but eventually made it home in one piece (more or less). The only damage was to my motorcycle seat, which now appeared to have a permanent pucker on it, for some unknown reason....

Back in the studio, I picked up where I had left off on the latest The Grafenberg Disciples album. I didn't think much more about that "Terra Incognita thingie"—until a few months later, Kevin called me out of breath and shouted in my ear, "I got it back! I got it back!"

After a few seconds of confusion, I realized what he was ranting about. The next words out of this mouth were, "Let's do this!"

...So It Begins

After a few days, the excitement was replaced by just one thought screaming in my head, "Oh Gawd, what have I done?" Nah, just kidding—I was raring to go. This was gonna be so much fun it would probably be illegal in several flyover states. First thing, I made calls to my songwriting team, Billy Connally and Jerry Merrill, to see if they were up for the task. They answered with a resounding Yes!

Hold on, I just realized you guys don't know who these folks are, so lemme introduce them.

Billy Connally (guitar) has been a friend of mine for nearly 45 years now. Even back in high school he could shred the guitar, but his real talent was much subtler; you see, Billy was a songwriter under all the widdleee-widdlleee guitar shredding. He had a grasp of song structure, hooks, and melody that far surpassed his young age. His mastery of songwriting only refined itself over the decades, and I couldn't think of a better partner for this project than Billy. It doesn't hurt that he's a master at baritone and seven-string chugging riffs. Yeah, he fit the bill nicely, and I knew he would be a pleasure to work with in the studio.

Next up is Jerry Merrill (keys). Jerry has been a friend for more than thirty years since we used to play in a Top 40 band in the late 80s. He is classically trained (so he knows, like, all the cool chords, man!) and is a chameleon on the keys, able to do anything from fusion, to rock, to Latin, to classical, to showtunes. I don't think there's a style he can't play. Plus, he plays what he calls "broken-world music," where he takes a piece and makes it just different (broken) enough that your ears perk up, and you wonder "What was that?" but without it being jarring or distracting. You can't ask for a better songwriting partner than one who knows all the music rules, yet takes a childish glee in breaking them. Jerry, too, was a perfect choice for this project.

Kevin and I were soon putting our heads together to create our dream lineup for the project. We bounced ideas around and quickly came up with some great choices for singers and guest artists. The majority of the basic tracks would be written and recorded by my songwriting team and members of The Grafenberg Disciples in my studio in Northern California. The guest tracks would be predominately recorded at the guest artists' home studios and "flown in" with the magic of technology.

The cast took final shape as:

Michael Sadler—Criston

Ted Leonard—Saan

Anneke Van Giersbergen—Ystya

Dan Reed—Prester Hannes

Hans Eberbach—Ondun

Guest Performers

Jonathan Dinklage—violin

Ed Toth—Drums

Gregg Bissonette—Drums

Jeff Tuttle—Drums

Jay Tausig—Nylon guitar

Jeffrey Wynn-Prince—12-string guitar

Emily Lynn—Background vocals (all)

Elizabeth Prince—vocal demos

Once we had our lineup under contract, Billy, Jerry, and I got together to start putting musical ideas down to a rough set of lyrics that Kevin provided us. In that first weekend songwriting retreat we wrote six songs for the album—not a bad couple days of work! Billy and Jerry went back home to Vancouver and Los Angeles, respectively, while I tried to make some sense of what we'd come up with.

A few weeks later Kevin flew to my studio in California to oversee what was going on, and I hoped to get his official okey dokey on what we had written. As we went through idea after idea, and Kevin kept bobbing his head in time with a big smile on his face, I could see we were near the mark. We just needed to polish and pump up those lyrics Kevin and his wife had drafted years ago in anticipation of doing a third album, but the songs had never been finished. Simply put, there just weren't enough words in those draft lyrics to fill out a proper Prog Rock song.

So, with some prodding by me, Kevin promised to go back home, corral Rebecca, and they would hunker down and get writing and expanding. After all the head bobbing and fun, as well as brainstorming and critiques, we finalized our plans.

That night, I took Kevin to see some friends of mine playing in a northern California Rush tribute band called RASH. After many beers and great comfort food, a good time was had by all. Kevin took pictures with the band and proclaimed them "Really Good" at the end of the night. Or at least that's what I thought he mumbled as he fell asleep in my car on the way home. (I did say many beers were had!)

One more songwriting session ensued a few months later, where Billy, Jerry, and I finished the album in a weekend. By this time I had a pretty good set of complete lyrics to work with, so I plunged in on the engineering stuff to get the songs out to the artists.

Only one track remained to be written. As I had read the trilogy, the biggest theme that caught my attention was how people exploit religion for their own goals, warping something arguably good into something that can only be described as evil. I kept thinking of its relevance to our planet today. This musing resulted in a new Grafenberg song, "Not in My Name." In recording it, the protagonist sounded like Ondun to me. I approached Kevin and asked him if pwetty, pwease, I could put one of my songs on the album, and he graciously agreed. "Not in My Name" is definitely a Grafenburg tune, but I licensed it to this album because it fits so well. Kevin agrees.

Fun fact about this tune: there are two versions. A Roswell 6 version and a Grafenberg Disciples version. The only difference is that the Roswell 6 version is more polite. I'll just leave it at that.....

I won't bore you with the technical blow-by-blow of how the songs were recorded. (That's only for die-hard tech geeks.) Honestly, there were lots of hiccups along the way, including a three-month stretch where no work got done due to computer issues that Apple couldn't figure out. (You listening, Apple?)

But I will say this. For a year, I was a kid in a candy store in my studio, receiving tracks from all over the world—Vancouver, Los Angeles, New York, St Louis, Prague, London, and Amsterdam. Each day brought a new surprise, delight, and challenge. I wouldn't change the experience for the world.

Every performer on this album played with passion and professionalism. Each elevated their song(s) higher with every track they added. It was a heady experience watching Kevin's vision come to life. When working with the artists, I can honestly say I encountered no strife—no divas, no attitudes, zip, zilch, nada. This is the way record making is supposed to be.

. . .

OKAY, I'll be honest with y'all. This is by far the biggest project I have ever undertaken. Truth to tell, it's a weird feeling for a producer to step into a project when its two-thirds complete with the responsibility to take the project across the finish line in a way that respects and pays homage to what has gone before and still somehow make it your own. I was very lucky in that very early on Kevin had told me not to make this a "Norlander" or a "Pauly" production; he wanted me to make it a "Madsen production." This is a perfect example of the adage, "Be careful what you wish for!" (Poor man, I really don't think Kevin knew what he was letting loose on the world!)

I want to thank Kevin for his amazing (insane?) faith in lil ol' me. Without getting into an Oscars speech here, I do want to take a moment to thank my family for putting up with all my incessant talking about the project for a year. (I couldn't tell anyone else! It was super top secret!) But I really want to point out someone special who kept propping me up and encouraging me, telling me this was my best work yet. Thank you Dale Titus for support above and beyond. (It's a little known fact, Dale has his own species named for him, "Supporticus Superious," a rare cousin of some salamander in Brazil with a penchant for UGG boots....)

So that's it. That's my story and I'm sticking to it. Kevin even told me I could have 3000 words, so to quote one of my favorite Canadian philosophers and orators (Rush fans will get this): "blah, blah,

blah, blah. Neener, neener, neener—that's 3,000 words.

—Bob Madsen, Northern California